Tucker Tales
Retriever Dreams

Written by **Vanessa J. Hampton**
Illustrated by **Judith Carruthers**

AuthorHouse™
1663 Liberty Drive
Bloomington, IN 47403
www.authorhouse.com
Phone: 1-800-839-8640

Published by AuthorHouse 02/18/2012

ISBN:978-1-4685-4914-0 (sc)

Library of Congress Control Number: 2012902155

This book is printed on acid-free paper.

authorHOUSE®

We've moved all morning,
and I should rest.

Jack, my playmate, will
snuggle close to my chest.

Theo, the cat,
will find a place on the mat.

Now, when I sleep—
in my dreams—
I can do as I wish
and move how I please.

I imagine I'm a dancer,
jumping forward and back.

Perhaps, Rudolph, the prancer,
leaving a strange track ...

Perhaps a gymnast, bouncing
up and down ...

... or a mouse walking backward
sporting a frown.

I can twist my feet under my seat ...

... and

scratch like a cat reaching its back.

I imagine I'm skating, sliding into a space ...
... straight and curved, spinning in place.

My pathway is a journey of straight
lines that change.

The zigzags ...

In my sleep
I can roll stretched like a log
or tight as a ball ...

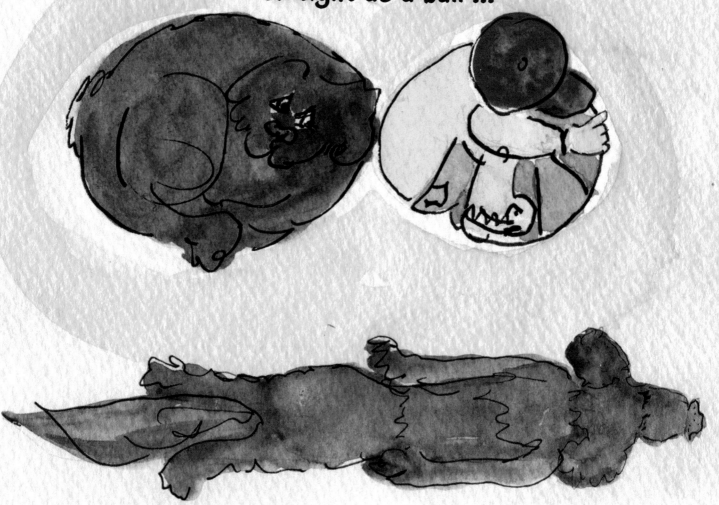

... then stretch my legs out and crawl.

I dream I can hop and skip,
in fact, do most any trick,
even a backward flip.

Sometimes I pretend I'm Jack,
skipping forward and back.
Step-hop,
        step-hop,
                step-hop.

I'm exhausted from this play.

I **NEED** to nap so I can scheme.
I'll close my eyes and dream.

Wasn't I already asleep?

Probing Questions

A challenge to stimulate observation, comprehension, and listening skills.

- What did Tucker dream he could wear on his head?
- What animal do you think Rudolph is?
- In Tucker's dreams, which animal frowned?
- Do you like to roll or jump?
- Have you ever dreamt about a puppy?
- What is it called when you step-hop, step-hop?
- Have you ever watched an animal sleep?
- What dreams do you think a mouse has?
- What do you dream about?

Coloring Page

Author: Vanessa J. Hampton

Vanessa Hampton was born in England and spent thirty-five years teaching in the area of her first love: health and movement education. She was voted the Vermont Association of Health, Physical Education, Recreation and Dance Teacher of the Year in 1993 and 2005.

She lives in Vermont and is married with two children. Her interests include watercolor and acrylic painting, dysautonomia and migraine research, kayaking, and snowshoeing.

Illustrator: Judith Carruthers

Born in Canada, Judith became a working illustrator at the age of fourteen. Several exhibits in Canada and the United States have highlighted Judith's comedic illustrations. She works with several forms of media including watercolor, pen and ink, pastels, acrylics, oil, and gouache.

She has two children and two grandchildren and lives in Vermont.

A portion of profits will be donated to
The Dysautonomia Information Network and The Wildland Firefighter Foundation.

CPSIA information can be obtained
at www.ICGtesting.com
Printed in the USA
LVIC030436100312

272494LV00002B